D0601753

CALGARY PUBLIC LIBRARY
APRIL 2018

IMPRINT

A part of Macmillan Publishing Group, LLC
175 Fifth Avenue, New York, NY 10010

ABOUT THIS BOOK

The artist's medium is digital. The text was set in Cheltenham,
and the display type is Garden Pro. The book was edited by Erin Stein
and art directed by Natalie C. Sousa. The production was supervised by
Raymond Ernesto Colón, and the production editor was Alexei Esikoff.

FIREFLY FOREST. Copyright © 2018 by Robyn Frampton. All rights reserved.

Printed in China by R. R. Donnelley Asia Printing Solutions Ltd,
Dongguan City, Guangdong Province.

Library of Congress Control Number: 2017945050

ISBN 978-1-250-12263-6 (hardcover)

Our books may be purchased in bulk for promotional, educational, or business use.
Please contact your local bookseller or the Macmillan Corporate and
Premium Sales Department at (800) 221-7945 ext. 5442 or by
e-mail at MacmillanSpecialMarkets@macmillan.com.

Imprint logo designed by Amanda Spielman
Book design by Liz Casal

First edition—2018

1 3 5 7 9 10 8 6 4 2

mackids.com

Fireflies fancy the fairest of fair.
So please do not steal; they prefer that you share.
Their message can be found on the pages within.
Their lights shine brighter when you
share with your friends.

ROBYN FRAMPTON

Firefly Forest

ILLUSTRATED BY MIKE HEATH

{Imprint}
MAKE YOUR MARK

New York

Beyond the veil of fireflies...

in the middle of your busy city,

hides a forest both charming and pretty.

There in the glade, past the old hollow tree,

Firefly Forest can set your heart free.

When you feel lost
or forgotten or down,
look for the Forest.
It wants to be found.

Under and between the shimmering leaves
ring friendly chuckles from magical beings.

They are hidden to any untrained eye;
they whisper around you sweet lullabies.

You've not been forgotten, is what they say.

We heard you calling and came right away.

We're here to help you and happy to stay.

We love you....
We'll lift you....
You'll find your way.

You are much stronger than
you think you are.
You're not alone.
We will never be far.

the giving tree

Whatever you need is what you will find
among the green ferns and the fireflies.

Once you have felt their warmth, kindness, and grace,

carry it with you when you leave this place.

Share the magic in the big world out there.
Reach out to someone and show them you care.

Show kindness and love in all that you do,
just as the Firefly Forest did for you.

THERE WAS A REAL FIREFLY FOREST IN A PARK IN KANSAS that I built anonymously, piece by piece. Like a magical seed, a tiny red door I fixed in the hollow of an oak tree brought the forest to life and it flourished by the power of kindness. Visitors were drawn into the forest hoping to catch a glimpse of the inhabitants. It became a place of connection, a place of belonging, a place to dream, a place to find relief, and a place to find hope. It became a mystery to the local news and eventually led to a short documentary film, *The Gnomist*, directed and produced by Sharon Liese.

While Firefly Forest began as a physical manifestation of my imagination running wild, my role as its creator was not to project my fantasy, dream, or belief onto others. Instead, I sought to build a magical space, hoping to ignite the imagination of those who happened upon it. A place where visitors felt they had discovered a hidden treasure that they were meant to find.

My experience in Firefly Forest was extraordinary. Though I no longer live in Kansas, the magic lives in me, and I continue to look for opportunities to share it with those around me. I believe that as we share the very best of ourselves with others, we can make the world a better place—that by using our individual talents and abilities, each one of us has the power to lift another up and make a difference.

SHARE YOUR MAGIC.

—ROBYN FRAMPTON

fireflyforestdoors.com

Adam M. Scott

ROBYN FRAMPTON is the creative force behind the mystery of Firefly Forest. In the spring of 2013, she began the project as part of her personal journey toward hope and healing. A self-taught carpenter, she individually carved and placed each door with the help of her young sons along a well-traveled, picturesque trail in the heart of America. Their anonymous efforts brought local residents together, dramatically affecting both the community and their own family by offering peace, joy, and hope.

Robyn and her sons now reside in Utah, where she recently graduated summa cum laude with a bachelor's degree in psychology. She continues to create magical spaces, most recently donating an enormous whimsical tree to Primary Children's Hospital in Salt Lake City. Her work was featured in the award-winning documentary *The Gnomist*, directed and produced by Sharon Liese and distributed by CNN Films in December 2015.

Mike Heath | Magnus Creative

MIKE HEATH communicates with pictures and is currently living out his passion to create through Magnus Creative with photo illustration. He graduated from Colorado State University in 2000 with a degree in fine arts, concentrating in photography and graphic design. After working as a designer and an art director for various publications, his photography evolved with his projects for both magazine spreads and bestselling authors. All of his work is created with location and studio photography, coupled with 3-D rendering when something simply doesn't exist. He is most inspired when exploring the beauty of Colorado and beyond with his wife and three children.